First American Edition 1999 by Kane/Miller Book Publishers
Brooklyn, New York & La Jolla, California

Originally published in Spain under the Catalan title *El Regal*
(*The Present*) by La Galera, S.A. Editorial, Barcelona, Spain in 1996

Library of Congress Cataloging-1n-Publication Data

Keselman, Gabriela.
[Regal. English]
The gift / by Gabriela Keselman ; Illustrated by Pep Montserrat ;
translated by Laura McKenna. — 1st American ed.
p. cm.
"A Cranky Nell book."
Summary: Mikie's birthday is coming and his parents cannot
figure out what to do when he tells them that he wants
something big, strong, smooth, sweet, warm, funny, and long-lasting.
[1. Gifts—Fiction. 2. Birthdays—Fiction. 3. Parent and child-Fiction.]
I. Montserrat, Pep, ill. II. McKenna, Laura. III. Title.
PZ7.K4813Gi   1999   [E]—dc21   99-17619

ISBN 0-916291-91-X
Printed and bound in Singapore by Tien Wah Press Pte. Ltd.
2 3 4 5 6 7 8 9 10

The Gift

The Gift

WRITTEN BY

Gabriela Keselman

ILLUSTRATED BY

Pep Montserrat

Translated by Laura McKenna

A CRANKY NELL BOOK

Kane/Miller Book Publishers

Mr. and Mrs. Goodparents were sitting in their Thinking Chair.

They only sat there when they had to think about something really important.

Today they were thinking about what to give their son Mikie for his birthday.

They thought and thought.

But the Thinking Chair was kind of hard.

Thinking was hard too.

So hard that after a while Mr. and Mrs. Goodparents
had three problems:

A pain in their bottoms,

A pain in their heads,

And still not a single idea.

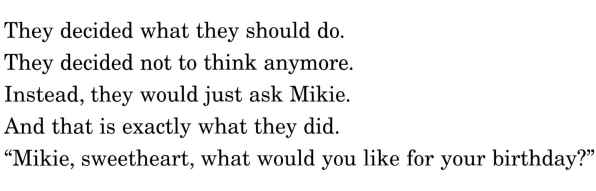

They decided what they should do.

They decided not to think anymore.

Instead, they would just ask Mikie.

And that is exactly what they did.

"Mikie, sweetheart, what would you like for your birthday?"

"I want a very special present!" Mikie answered.
"And I want it to be very . . .

BIG!

"He wants an elephant!"

Mr. and Mrs. Goodparents grabbed each other's hands.

"And I want it to be very . . .

SOFT!

Mr. and Mrs. Goodparents touched noses.

"And I want it to be very . . .

SWÈÈT !

Mr. and Mrs. Goodparents stepped on each other's toes.

"And I want it to be . . .

WARM! VERY WARM!

Mr. and Mrs. Goodparents pinched each other's cheeks.

"And also," Mikie insisted,

I want it to rock from side to side!

Mr. and Mrs. Goodparents felt quite dizzy.

"And I want it to make me *fly* too!"

Mr. and Mrs. Goodparents froze like statues.

"And I want it to make me . . .

laugh!

Mr. and Mrs. Goodparents fell over.

"And I want it to last a loooong time!!"

Mr. and Mrs. Goodparents were beside themselves.

In truth, they were very confused. The gift had to be BIG,   **STRONG**,

And it had to ROCK from side to side, make him *FLY*, make him *LAUGH*,

SOFT,  SWEET and WARM.

and last a very **loooong** time. Where would they find such a special gift?

It wasn't an easy question.
So, they went back to their Thinking Chair.
They sat and thought, but it didn't do any good.
They couldn't think of an answer.
A day passed. And then two. And then three.

Finally the big day arrived! Mr. and Mrs. Goodparents still had
not thought of a gift for Mikie.
They felt terrible.
They got up from their Thinking Chair and went to find him.

"Mikie, sweetheart . . . ,"
the Goodparents said in a very sad voice.
"Ah, eh, er . . .
We haven't found . . .
cough, cough . . .
the gift . . .

er, hmmmm . . .
you wanted . . ."

And since they didn't know what else to say, they gave him a **BIG**, **STRONG**, *SOFT*, *SWĖĖT*, WARM hug.

Then they rocked him from side to side, *tossed* him up in the air and made him *laugh* for a **looooong** time.